BRAVE HEARTS
The Lavender Fairies
#1

Piper Punches

Original Illustrations
Evelyn Schmidt

Brave Hearts is a work of fiction. Names, characters, place, and incidents either are the product of the author's imagination or are used fictitiously. Any resemblance to actual persons, living or dead, events, or locales is entirely coincidental.

Copyright @ 2018 Piper Punches

ISBN: 978-0-9910936-8-7

All rights reserved.
No part of this book may be reproduced, scanned or distributed in any printed or electronic form without permission. Please do not participate or encourage piracy of copyrighted materials in violation of the author's rights.

First Published in the United States in 2018.

Cover Design: Martin Hammond
Cover Art: Evelyn Schmidt
Tree Image: Pixabay
House Image: Pixabay

For inquiries, please contact the author directly at:
http://piperpunches.com
piper@piperpunches.com

*To All Who Believe In the
Power of Magic and a Kind Heart*

~R & C, K &K~

Contents

1.	A Sweet Surprise	7
2.	Emily Shares a Secret	14
3.	The Magical Grove	22
4.	Ali Has a Plan	30
5.	The Loose Tooth	34
6.	The Tooth Fairy	37
7.	Fairy Hope	41
8.	Operation Fairy Rescue	44
9.	Brave Hearts	46
10.	Friends Forever	53
	Meet the Lavender Fairies	57
	Create Your Own Story	59

Chapter One
A Sweet Surprise

Emily loves sunset on her family's lavender farm. She loves how bright orange and soft purple colors paint the sky. But her favorite sunset color is blushing pink.

Walking in the lavender fields at sunset is Emily's favorite time for another reason too. In the evening she walks between the plants, inhaling the sweet, sharp scent and doesn't worry about the bees.

The bees are Emily's enemies.

If the bees sting, she gets sick. Then her mom gets scared and has to use the special weapon against the bees. Emily thinks it is funny - strange funny - that something so small, like an itty-bitty bee, can be so dangerous.

But she doesn't let it worry her too much. During the warm days of spring, summer, and early autumn, she stays inside and helps her mom create yummy-smelling soaps that they sell online. There are times when she gets a little sad and the jealousy bug bites her. Those are the times when she spies Ethan running around outside, the sunshine on his face and a happy, cheerful smile on his lips.

Then she remembers. She remembers nighttime is her time when she enjoys the farm alone.

Except tonight she is not alone.

First, she hears the *swish-zip* sound next to her ear. *Swish-zip, swish-zip.* Next, her nose picks up the scent of English lavender and baby powder. And, now, she sees an orange light zig-zagging between the rows of Royal Velvet lavender.

She wishes she had her firefly jar with her.

The light bounces up and down, hovering in one spot. Emily gets down on her hands and knees. She crawls toward the light.

"I bet you're a big firefly. The biggest in the world."

The closer Emily gets the slower the light bounces and the stronger the delightful smell becomes. When she's close enough, she reaches out her hand and swipes at the lighting bug. She only catches air and hears a giggle.

Emily stands up quickly. "Who's there?"

No one answers.

She looks back at the house to see if Ethan has followed her outside. She sees him through the back window, sitting at the kitchen table, putting a puzzle together with their dad.

Another giggle.

Emily searches the tops of the lavender blooms for the orange light.

"Over here."

Emily crawls farther into the garden. "Who's there?"

"Me, of course."

The orange light is in front of Emily now. She feels a tickle on her hand then the light gets brighter. Inside the light is a little girl with wings and short, curly, yellow hair pulled back with a headband. Emily flings her hands to the sky, yelps and falls back onto her heels.

The fairy girl giggles and flies around Emily's head before landing on the girl's dirty knees.

"Who? What are you?"

"My name is Abriali Lavender. But call me Ali. It's easier for humans to say. You're Emily."

"How do you know that?"

The fairy shrugs. "I know everything. Your name is Emily Zink. That little human boy, who wakes me up during the day, is Ethan Zink. He's your brother."

Emily nods.

"I have a brother too. His name is Dilly-Dilly. He's

silly like your brother."

"Why haven't I seen you before?" Emily asks.

"You weren't looking for me."

"Oh. That makes sense." Emily rubs her eyes to make sure she's seeing what she's seeing. It's getting darker.

She knows her mom will come looking for her soon. Will she see Ali? She hopes not. She wants to keep her to herself.

"You have to go."

"What?"

"You have to go. Your mom is getting ready to walk this way. She's rinsing her tea cup and then she'll come looking for you."

"But -"

"I told you, Emily. I know everything about humans. But come back tomorrow night?"

"Okay."

Ali turns her light back on. "Great! Bring your silly brother."

"Um, okay." She does not want to bring Ethan, but she doesn't feel she has a choice.

"Great! I need your help with something Emily. I can count on you, right?"

Emily tries to smile, but she frowns instead. She is so confused.

"Yes. I promise. I'll be here tomorrow night with Ethan."

Brave Hearts (Lavender Fairies Series, Book 1)

"Great! See you then." Ali and her bouncy, yellow hair fly away.

Chapter Two
Emily Shares a Secret

The next night it takes forever to finish dinner. Emily complains of a stomachache and pushes her plate of spaghetti away from her.

"Do you need to lie down?" her mom asks.

Emily shakes her head and reaches for her glass of

water. She watches Ethan slurp his noodles then reach for the hot sauce next to his plate.

"That's so gross," Emily says.

Ethan shrugs and dribbles it over the meat sauce. Their dad snickers and shakes his head. "My crazy kids. I love you both so much."

"We love you, too, Dad. Hey, Ethan," Emily grins at him. "Want to walk with me tonight?"

Her brother's brown eyes grow huge and a smile spreads across his face. Emily knows she won't have to bribe him with her dessert to get him to follow. All Ethan ever wants to do is be with her. Every night he asks to come with her, but she tells him no.

It is her special alone time.

It is her magic. And, although she is smiling too, she is not happy about sharing the magic with him, but she wants to make Ali happy.

"Can I, Mom? Dad?" Ethan is on his knees, rocking the kitchen chair back and forth. His excitement makes the table shake.

"Sit down, little man, "says his dad.

"Can I?"

"Of course," says his mom. "Listen to your sister and don't run through the rows. We want healthy plants, not plants smashed from little feet. Got it?"

"Got it!" Ethan stands. "Ready?"

"Wait," their mom says. "Emily, I thought you didn't feel good?"

"I'm better now."

"Hmm, I see. Well, we eat our dinner before dessert. So, if you're hungry later your dinner plate will be waiting for you."

"Yes, Mom." Emily walks around the table and takes Ethan's hand. "Ready?"

Ethan stays by his sister's side not getting ahead. He is talking fast, spitting out words like he hasn't talked in days.

"Ethan."

"Yeah?"

"I have a secret."

"A secret?" he asks, loudly.

"Ssh."

"Sorry," he whispers. "What's the secret?"

"Come here." She leads Ethan to the spot where

she saw the orange light the night before. Tonight there isn't a light. Emily points to the ground. "Sit down."

Ethan frowns. He doesn't like it when she tells him what to do.

"Please?"

He sits with his legs tucked under him. "What's the secret?"

Emily smells the familiar scent. "Do you smell that?"

Ethan nods. "It smells good."

"It smells like a fairy," Emily says.

"Hi!" Ali drops down between the two children, smiling very big.

"AHHH!" Ethan screams and swats at Ali.

The fairy giggles and wags her finger at the little boy. "Be careful, silly boy. I just had my wings shined today. You have to keep your human fingers to yourself."

Ethan grabs his sister's arm and buries his face in her elbow. She pats him on his head.

"It's okay. This is Ali. She's my secret. Our secret."

He looks at Ali between squinty eyes then buries his head in his sister's elbow again.

"It's nice to meet you, Ethan." Ali flutters between him and Emily before landing on a mound of dirt.

"How do you know my name?"

The fairy and Emily look at each other and smile. "Fairies know everything about humans," Emily tells her brother.

"Darn tootin' we do!" says a voice from behind the lavender bush.

"Come out, Dilly-Dilly," Ali says, giggling and smiling.

The boy fairy stands in front of Ethan. His fists are on each of his hips and he frowns. "We know everything and we don't need human help."

"Another one?" Ethan whispers.

"This is my brother, Dilly-Dilly, and, yes, we do need their help," Ali says, giving her brother a stern look.

"Humph! This one," the boy fairy points his finger at Ethan, "is scared of us. How is he going to help us get rid of the spittlebugs?"

"Stop it. We need their help," says Ali.

"What are spittlebugs?" Emily asks.

"They are nasty, little bugs who are taking over our village," Dilly answers.

"Oh, no! They sound horrible."

Ali shrugs. "Well, they don't mean to be. Our homes are the lavender bushes and that's the only food for the spittlebugs here. They're just hungry. Can we blame them?"

"Humph! Yes, we can," Dilly-Dilly says. "That lazy spittle, Fire, ate part of my window last night. And, Mimi? She left all her gooey-goo behind on the rest of the window."

"Calm down, Dilly. I have a plan, but we need some bigger help."

"What's gooey-goo?" Ethan asks.

Dilly-Dilly shakes his head and his blue hair falls over his eyes. "See, Ali. He doesn't know anything."

"Do so!" Ethan shouts.

"Do not!" Dilly-Dilly shouts back.

"Stop," Emily says. She taps Ethan on the

Piper Punches

shoulder. "Can you keep this secret?"

Ethan is glaring at Dilly-Dilly but nods. Ali buzzes around their heads and giggles. "Yay!"

"So, what *is* gooey-goo?" Emily asks.

Ali lands on Emily's shoulder. "It's foam that

hides them when they eat and sleep. It's their home, really."

"Oh, so do you have a plan?"

"Oh, so do you have a plan?" Dilly-Dilly copies Emily and rolls his eyes. "Of course, we have a plan. Right Ali?"

Ali smiles. "You bet we do! Follow me."

Chapter Three
The Magical Grove

"I don't like this," Ethan whispers to Emily. They're following Ali's orange light and Dilly-Dilly's green light. "I think they want to eat us."

Emily laughs and ruffles her little brother's hair. "Eat us? How? Look how much bigger we are."

"So? Maybe they'll cast a magic spell on us that

makes us teeny-tiny like them. You think about that?"

"Ethan."

"What?"

"That's not going to happen. You're not afraid of the tooth fairy. What's the difference?"

"The tooth fairy is just different. Besides, she brings me money. Are we going to get money for helping Ali and what's-his-face?"

"I doubt it, but I promise nothing will happen."

The fairies' orange and green lights stop at the edge of the field where the forest begins. The sun has disappeared from the sky and the after-glow is starting to fade. Even Emily hesitates to go any farther. The forest at night is scary. It is too dark and they are not allowed.

"Can we do this when it's day?" Emily asks.

Ali shakes her head. "We sleep during the day. We don't want humans to mistake us for butterflies and try to catch us."

"It's bad enough that you try to put us in jars at night because you think we're fireflies. We are so much cooler than fireflies!" Dilly-Dilly exclaims.

Ali hovers in front of Emily and Ethan. "Come with us. Let me show you what I built."

The two human siblings follow the fairy siblings into the woods. In the distance, Emily hears her mom call for them, but she keeps going into the forest. When she enters the woods, there is a section without many trees and in that clearing is a glowing sphere, a big ball of light. Emily and Ethan walk closer. Ethan holds his sister's hand tightly.

"I call it Spittlebug Land. I made it two nights ago."

"What is it?" Emily asks.

"It's a magical grove."

"What's a grove?" Ethan asks.

"It's like an apple tree field," Ali tells him.

"I don't see any apples," he says, unsure.

"Of course not, "says Ali, covering her mouth to stop a giggle from escaping. "This is a lavender grove that's just for the spittlebugs. Come closer."

They walk closer to the glowing ball. They can see into it. Inside the ball, they see a beautiful garden

Brave Hearts (Lavender Fairies Series, Book 1)

with all types of different lavender. The bushes are green and overflowing with blooms.

"It's bigger inside than it looks out here."

"Can we go in?" Ethan asks.

"Aren't you scared?" Dilly-Dilly asks.

Ali shakes her head. "No. You can't go in because you don't have the right magic."

"What type of magic is that?" Emily asks.

"The fairy type," Ali says. "But trust us. It's a beautiful grove where the lavender bushes grow all day, every day. It's a paradise and it's just for the spittlebugs."

"But Mimi, Fire, and their brothers, Pepper and Liam, won't leave our farm and come here on their own," says Dilly-Dilly.

"Why not?" Emily can't imagine who wouldn't want to live in a magical place.

Ali shrugs. "I think they're scared."

"I think they like the way my window tastes," Dilly-Dilly says, crossing his arms and frowning.

"Whatever the reason," Ali says. "We have to get them out of here fast and my magic won't work to get them to leave. They're destroying our homes."

"There's more of you?" Ethan asks.

Ali nods. Her eyes grow wide and sparkle. "Oh

yes! My mom and dad, all of our cousins, some aunts and uncles, and then the traveling fairies. We even have a guest house for Tooth Fairy when she comes to visit you."

"Oh my goodness," Ethan whispers. "Emily, how come we've never seen them?"

Emily smiles and winks at Ali. "Because we haven't been looking."

"Emily and Ethan! What are you doing?" Their mom walks into the grove, stepping dangerously close to Spittlebug Land. The light from the flashlight in her hand bounces up and down.

Ali whispers in Emily's ear, "Don't worry she can't see Dilly-Dilly and I."

The lights go out on the sphere. The fairies stay still.

"Why are you two in the woods? You know you're supposed to stay close to the house."

"Mom, guess what?" Ethan says, excited. Emily pinches him. "Ow!"

"Sorry, Mom. We were playing a game and didn't realize how far away we were."

Their mom shines the flashlight around the area and frowns. Does she smell them, Emily wonders? If she does, she doesn't say anything. "Well, you need to come in. It's bath time."

"I can't wait to come back here tomorrow night!" Ethan says, jumping up and down.

"Nope," their mom says. "Not tomorrow night or the next night. Since I can't trust the two of you to stay by the house, you get a time out from the fields for the next two nights."

"Two nights!" The siblings cry out. Emily hears Ali and Dilly-Dilly repeat the same thing.

"Yes, two nights. Now let's go."

Their mom shines the flashlight away from the woods and motions for them to follow. As they leave, Emily and Ethan hear Dilly-Dilly say, "Great! Two more nights of spittlebug gooey-goo on our homes. They'll probably eat my door next."

Brave Hearts (Lavender Fairies Series, Book 1)

Chapter Four
Ali Has A Plan

Ali and Dilly-Dilly follow the human girl and boy to the edge of the lavender field and watch them go into the house.

"Now what?" asks Dilly-Dilly.

"We have to tell them our plan."

"I know, but how? We can't go near the house."

Ali flips her orange light on and off. She does this when she thinks and when she gets nervous. "Maybe we can just this one time."

Dilly-Dilly flies in front of Ali, pointing his stubby fairy finger at her face. "No! We will get in trouble if we do. Dad will know."

Ali knows he is right. Their dad, Wooly Lavender, is a kind, gentle man with one rule: No going near the humans' home. He agreed to let his children contact the human girl when she came into the field, but he's absolutely forbidden them to go near the house.

"It's too risky," he said. "What if one of you gets caught? My magic doesn't work outside the lavender fields. You'd be stuck in a jar forever."

Ali flutters over to her thinking swing made from a hawk's feather and tied between two branches. She swings back and forth, scratching her head and wrinkling her nose. Dilly-Dilly goes over to the side of their house and starts poking at the gooey-goo. This wakes up Fire, who presses his nose against the foam and then sticks his tongue out at his fairy nemesis.

Dilly-Dilly turns away from Fire's teasing. He joins his sister. "Anything yet?"

"Maybe. Did you notice that the boy kept touching his tongue to his tooth?"

"Yeah?"

"Are you thinking what I'm thinking?"

"Yeah, well, no because I never know what you're thinking, Ali. Also, I'm hungry and I'm thinking about food."

"You always think about food. I'm thinking that Ethan's loose tooth is just what we need to tell them our plan."

Chapter Five
The Loose Tooth

"Emily!"

Emily drops the book she is reading. She is up on her feet when Ethan slides into the living room on his socked feet. He stands in front of her grinning and holding out his hand. In the middle of his palm is a tiny, white tooth.

"It came out," Ethan says.

"That's great, buddy," Emily smiles and sits back down with her book. She has been in a bummer mood since their parents grounded them. Ethan on the other hand has not been too bothered. He has spent the last two hours building a fort in the basement and wiggling that silly tooth non-stop. All his hard work has finally paid off.

"I'm going to put it under my pillow right now."

"That's a good idea."

"And then I'm going to bed."

"We haven't eaten dinner yet."

Ethan shrugs. "But I'm sooooo sleepy." He fake yawns and bounds up the stairs to his room.

"What was that about?" her mom asks. She sits down next to Emily on the couch.

"He lost that tooth."

"Wow! I thought it was never going to come out. Is that a good book?"

"It's okay."

"Is something bothering you?" asks her mom.

"I just miss my nighttime walks in the field."

"I know you do, sweetie. Believe me, I know how much you enjoy those walks. But when I couldn't find you, well, that scared me. Your father and I love you so much. We don't want anything to happen to you."

"I promise not to scare you again."

Her mom puts her arms around her and pulls her into a big bear hug. "I'm not sure that's a promise you can keep. Parents get scared. It's our job."

"Mom?"

"Yeah?"

"You might want to check on Ethan. He's so excited for the tooth fairy to come that he's already went to bed."

Her mom laughs. "That silly nut. I better go tell him I made his favorite spaghetti for dinner."

Emily wrinkles her nose. "With hot sauce?"

"Don't worry. I made grilled cheese sandwiches for us."

Chapter Six
The Tooth Fairy

"Wake up."

Emily hears the voice whisper in her ear, but she grabs her pillow and puts it over her head.

"Wake up!"

Ethan's voice gets louder and he is pushing on Emily's shoulders. She throws the pillow off the bed and sits up. The moon is high in the sky. "It's the middle of the night."

"Look." He hands Emily a letter and a flashlight.

She reads the letter and rereads it again.

"She gave me $1 and *us* this letter. I can't read all the words."

Dear Emily and Ethan,

I'm sorry we got you in trouble. Will you still help us? If yes, please bring a bucket, a rope, and your bravest heart.

Love,

Ali and Dilly-Dilly

"What do you think?" Emily asks Ethan. "Still want to help?"

"You bet!"

"Yay! Okay, but now you need to go to sleep."

Ethan sits on the edge of his sister's bed and rubs his belly. "I'm not sure I can. I don't think my tummy likes spaghetti and hot sauce anymore."

Emily hands Ethan a blanket from the end of her

Brave Hearts (Lavender Fairies Series, Book 1)

bed and another pillow from her chair in the corner. "Will a sleepover help?"

Ethan's eyes brighten and he nods. "You bet!"

Chapter Seven
Fairy Hope

Ali sees the light coming from Emily's window and gets excited. Her wings start flapping super-fast.

"What's wrong?" Dilly-Dilly asks.

"I think they got the letter."

"Are you sure you can trust Tooth Fairy. She's kinda forgetful. Remember when Emily was five and Tooth Fairy didn't show up for two whole days?"

Ali shakes her head. "Why do you always have to be so gloomy?"

"I'm not gloomy."

"Whatever. But Tooth Fairy delivered the letter. I know she did. Why else would Emily's light be on this late?"

Ali has spent many nights watching the Zink household from her perch high atop her home. She's watched the little human girl since they first moved into the farmhouse five years ago. Dilly-Dilly doesn't trust humans, but Ali thinks they are their own type of magic. She has wanted to be Emily's friend forever.

The light stays on in Emily's room for fifteen minutes then goes off.

"Do you hear that?" Dilly-Dilly asks.

Ali listens carefully. The sound is tiny, but she hears it - *slurp, tsk, slurp, tsk*. It's the sound of Fire and his brothers and sister destroying the homes in the village. Even though Fire likes to taunt Dilly-

Dilly, making faces and creating foam, he is not trying to be mean. He is just being a spittlebug, but Ali and the rest of the lavender fairies need them to do it somewhere else.

Dilly-Dilly flutters over to his side and begins snoring softly. Ali looks back at the farmhouse. She hopes Tooth Fairy came through and that her new human friends will help them get the spittlebugs to their new home. If they can't, Ali, her brother, her parents, and the rest of the lavender fairies will have to leave.

Ali does not want to leave. This is the only home she has ever known. She can't imagine living anywhere else. The human children are their last hope.

Chapter Eight
Operation Fairy Rescue

The school day was so long. Emily tried to pay attention to her teacher, but she kept thinking about tonight. When the last bell rang, she ran out of the classroom and waited for Ethan by the bus.

"Are you ready?" Emily asks.

"I don't know."

"Why?"

"I don't think that boy fairy likes me."

"Dilly-Dilly?"

"Yeah. He's always making stinky faces at me."

Emily laughs. "I think he's just cranky. Sounds like he isn't sleeping well because those spittlebugs are causing problems. They really need our help."

"I know. We can use my Lego bucket. I dumped it out this morning."

"Great! I dug a jump rope out from the toy chest. What about the brave heart?"

Ethan looks down at his feet, takes a deep breath, and then looks at Emily. He touches his heart. "All ready."

Emily touches her own heart. "Me too."

"After dinner?" Ethan asks.

"Yup! First dinner and then Operation Fairy Rescue!"

She and Ethan give each other a high five then climb the bus stairs and head home.

Chapter Nine
Brave Hearts

"Are they coming?" Dilly-Dilly asks. He's standing behind a lavender stalk pulling gooey-goo from his wings. Fire covered the fairies' front door with the thick foam overnight. Dilly-Dilly spent all day freeing himself from the goo.

"I don't see them, but I hear them. Sounds like

they're finishing dinner. Their dad wants them to put their dishes away."

Dilly-Dilly sticks his finger in his ear. He pulls out a wad of goo. "I can't hear anything."

"Oh, I'm so nervous."

"It's going to work."

Ali twirls her hair between her fingers. "I hope. Here they come!"

The human children stand at the edge of the field. Ethan's dragging the bucket behind him. Ali's never been afraid of humans, but understands why her papa and others fear the giants. Their feet are big and their hands are huge. The humans don't know how dangerous they are to the things they can't see.

"You got our note," Ali says.

"That was smart," Emily says. "But we don't have a lot of time. We have to be back soon."

"Follow me," Ali says. She leads the way to where the Spittlebugs are sleeping.

Ethan puts his nose close to the foam. "I don't see them."

"Oh, they're in there," Dilly-Dilly says. They hide

Piper Punches

really well."

"What are we going to do?" Emily asks.

Ali and Dilly-Dilly fly over to their house and pull a blue, fairy-sized garden hose from behind the house.

"We don't want to destroy their home," Ali says. "We just have to wash it away so we can get them to their new home. But washing away the gooey-goo isn't enough. The Spittles are going to be scared.

They're going to hold on tight to the branches. The only way to get them to their new home is to carefully lift them from the branches, put them in the bucket, and take them to the grove."

"We have to touch them?" Ethan asks. His eyes grow big with fright.

Ali and Dilly-Dilly nod.

"The brave heart," Ethan says.

Emily takes his hand. She knows that Ethan doesn't like to touch bugs, frogs, butterflies, or any other creepy crawlies. He doesn't like the way their bodies feel in his little hands. It is Emily who loves getting close to nature.

"You've got this," Emily assures him.

Ethan nods. "Okay. But just this one time."

Ali smiles. "Yes! Just this once. Are you ready?"

Dilly-Dilly takes the hose and aims it at the gooey-goo. "This is going to feel so good. One . . . two . . . three!"

A stream of rainbow-colored water and glitter sprays from the hose. As soon as the magical water touches the foam, it begins to dissolve, and the spittlebugs are exposed.

They're so pretty, Emily thinks. The green bug with an orange stripe down his back she assumes is Fire. The other bugs, Mimi, Pepper, and Liam, are green but each one has a different color stripe: yellow, silver, and blue.

When all the foam dissolves, Emily and Ethan remove the bugs gently from the branches. Emily holds the green and blue bug in her hand. The frightened bug looks up at her with big eyes. "It's okay," Emily says. "I promise we won't hurt you."

Ethan holds the green and silver bug in his hand.

"That's Liam," Dilly-Dilly tells him.

"Hi, Liam," Ethan whispers. "You're kinda okay, I guess."

Very carefully Emily and Ethan put the spittlebugs in the bucket.

"Now what?" Ethan asks.

"We take them to the edge of the forest," Ali answers.

Emily hesitates. "Wait. We can't go back in the forest. We promised our mom and dad."

Ali nods. "I know. That's what the rope is for. Follow us and we'll show you."

"What should we do?" Ethan asks.

"Come on," Emily says, and they follow the fairies.

When they get to the edge of the forest, Ali tells them to put the bucket on the ground and tie the rope around it. "We'll take it from here."

The two fairies tug the bucket under the glowing sphere. Then, Ali and Dilly-Dilly flutter around and around the sphere.

"May you live happily forever in a home that always has food, love, and warmth," the fairies chant three times. While they speak the magical spell, a lavender cloud rises from the bucket and the spittlebugs jump up and down in the middle like it's a big, fluffy pillow. Emily's sure they are laughing.

The cloud slides right into the glowing ball that suddenly glows a deep pink.

Ali and Dilly-Dilly peek inside the ball and smile. "It worked!" Ali exclaims. "They look so happy." Emily and Ethan clap their hands and jump up and down.

"We couldn't have done it without you," Dilly-Dilly admits. "Thank you."

"Now what?" Emily asks.

Ali flies over to her and lands on her shoulder. "I think it's time to get back to your home. This time I'm paying attention and I hear your mom getting ready to call for you. Can you come back tomorrow night?"

Emily grins. "You bet!"

Chapter Ten
Friends Forever

"Did you sleep good last night?" Emily asks, laughing when Dilly-Dilly's wings tickle her ear. He's full of energy and buzzing around her head. Emily and Ethan are sitting between the rows of lavender watching the rest of the fairies buzz about. The colors are so pretty and vibrant. It's hard for

Emily to believe that her mom and dad can't see the light show in the field.

Ali nods. "We have a lot of cleanup to do. The Spittles definitely left behind a mess, but we don't have to worry about gooey-goo and dried up lavender bushes anymore."

"Is this the last time I'll see you?"

Emily couldn't sleep last night because she was afraid she wouldn't have Ali's friendship anymore. It's hard for Emily to make friends because she's quiet and prefers to read than talk. Having a friend like Ali makes her happy.

"I hope not! Right Dilly-Dilly?"

"Really?" Emily smiles. "I thought you'd disappear now."

"Disappear? No way. This is our home. That's why we tried so hard to protect it."

"Well, that's true," Emily says.

Ali hoovers in front of Emily and gives her a big smile. "Emily, you never have to worry. We're friends forever."

Friends forever. Emily likes that idea and she can't

Brave Hearts (Lavender Fairies Series, Book 1)

wait for her next adventure with the lavender fairies.

THE END . . . FOR NOW

Stay tuned for a new Lavender Fairies book soon!

-A Note for Parents-

Sign up to get updates when new Lavender Fairies books are published

http://bit.ly/lavenderfairies

Piper Punches

Brave Hearts (Lavender Fairies Series, Book 1)

Meet the Lavender Fairies

Abriali Lavender

Favorite Color
Purple

Favorite Trick
Making rainbows appear to cheer
humans up after a rainfall!

Tell more about the plant she's named after
Abriali lavender grows all year (perennial). It loves
the sun and attracts bees and butterflies. The
flowers can also be crystallized and used to
decorate desserts.

Dilly-Dilly Lavender

Favorite Color
Green

Favorite Trick
Playing hide and seek from the bunnies in the field.

Tell more about the plant he's named after

Dilly Dilly lavender is deer resistant and grows well in drought conditions. Unlike other lavender varieties, Dilly Dilly repels bees. It is very low maintenance and enjoys the heat.

Brave Hearts (Lavender Fairies Series, Book 1)

Want to Create Your Own Lavender Fairy Story?

Use the pages in this book to write or draw your very own lavender adventure!

_____

_____
_____
_____
_____
_____
_____
_____
_____
_____
_____
_____
_____
_____

Piper Punches

Brave Hearts (Lavender Fairies Series, Book 1)

Piper Punches

Brave Hearts (Lavender Fairies Series, Book 1)

Piper Punches

Brave Hearts (Lavender Fairies Series, Book 1)

Piper Punches

Brave Hearts (Lavender Fairies Series, Book 1)

Piper Punches

Brave Hearts (Lavender Fairies Series, Book 1)

Piper Punches

Brave Hearts (Lavender Fairies Series, Book 1)

Piper Punches

Brave Hearts (Lavender Fairies Series, Book 1)

Piper Punches

Brave Hearts (Lavender Fairies Series, Book 1)

Piper Punches

Brave Hearts (Lavender Fairies Series, Book 1)

Piper Punches

Brave Hearts (Lavender Fairies Series, Book 1)

Piper Punches

CPSIA information can be obtained
at www.ICGtesting.com
Printed in the USA
FSHW021136220519
58313FS